This book was written to empower young people to follow their dreams and stay positive in their beliefs.

Studd's Juke Joint

by

Jerry Powell

ISBN: 978-0-9883374-6-6

Cover Design: Brittany J. Jackson

Published by G Publishing, LLC

Printed in the United States of America

CONTENTS

INTRODUCTION

The Juke Joint was just the place for an exciting outing. Music, dancing, and games of chance were there for all to get pleasure from. Let's not forget all the fine looking partyers in attendance. During any nightly celebration at the Juke Joint, a person should try not to insult anybody. Misunderstandings could easily turn into fights. Every now and then, a customer's attitude became so ugly that that angry customer would bring out a knife or even a gun which would cause a terrible situation. However, at Studd's place those kinds of violent behaviors were not tolerated. Everyone knew Studd had a special relationship with the district's Sheriff's Department.

The Juke Joint's operation created profit for both parties. Fights would draw negative attention to the establishment, which was bad for business. Bad business meant that the public stayed away which in turn caused lower profits. Collin County is a dry county; no alcoholic beverages were to be sold in it. However, money talks if you knew the right hands to feed in this region of the state.

Without the protection of the Sheriff's office, jail time for Studd's operations surely would have ensued. Studd had business relationship with many powerful politicians plus he paid off a few deputies. However, if the Sheriff Deputies got involved because of a violent fight, it meant someone was going to jail. Jails for a man of color in Mississippi represented free chain gang hard labor to the County or State.

In Mississippi, during the 1920's, black people had problems of all kinds. Their living conditions were less than that of any other nationality. Jobs mostly consisted of hard labor, paying colored people much less than that of Caucasians for the same work done. Just looking in the wrong directions could

Jerry Powell

easily cause Negro men to lose their lives. A Negro male was not allowed to look eye to eye with Caucasian men out in the public streets. If a Negro man was accused by a Caucasian of looking at Caucasian women for a long period, all hell might break loose. Heaven forbid touching her anywhere. Beating that Negro in public, even killing him for that infraction could easily happen. Therefore, a lot of Negros was submissive to Caucasians. Many Negros would take out their frustration on each other for just about any little thing. Stepping on ones shined shoes could easily be reason for an altercation. Thank God for the Studd's Juke Joint. Happy days, happy days.

In a wooded area, in the northeastern corner of Collins Counties colored folks would come together at Studd's Juke Joint and party like there was no tomorrow. Dressed in their finest attire, dressed to impress, they came. As far away as 20 miles, they came looking for the right substance and situation to make them forget about their long hard work week each had endured. So! For many to envelop their various sorrows, alcohol and socializing with the opposite sex was often the substitute for forgetting problems.

This story tells how a young man becomes a successful business owner, in the back woods of Mississippi …

Chapter 1: **STARTING OUT**

George was the fourth child of eight children blessed to William and Viola Hicks-Freeman. He was educated at an early age of the importance of hands in the field. George was not allowed the chance to get much schooling in the public education system. His Poppa and Mama are Share-croppers and needed all hands in the fields to plant or harvest the crops. However, George did get enough schooling to learn the letters to sign his name. For some reason counting came easy for George. Math problems were no problem for George. He was able to figure them out quick and accurately. His parents recognized he had a gift, so harvest time became George's time.

After traveling a few times to the scales, where the weight of the picked crops exchanged hands for cash, George quickly had it figured out. George could calculate the total dollar amount per bail weight before the warehouse foreman had the chance to add up the numbers on paper. After a few times of seeing his son's mathematics skills, George's Poppa decided to send him to the product weight scales in charge of collecting the correct dollar amount for the picked crop. Being successful, George began to take care of all the family business at the warehouse. Seeing such a young boy handling his families' livelihood, George was quickly noticed by the warehouse's owner, Mr. Charles. Because of his math skills, George's father was told by Mr. Charles that George was too special to work out in the field and that he would be worth more to the family's income if he worked as a clerk at the warehouse. With individual training and under sudden conditions, George could really amount to something that the Color people in the area would be proud of. George's Poppa agreed to let George work at the warehouse for a set wage, which he would collect.

Jerry Powell

George had no say in the business matters, he just did as ordered.

George's training at the Warehouse ended up taking up more and more of his time. So much so, that he asked to sleep over in Mr. Charles's storeroom to save time in daily travel. Walking back and forward to his family cabin took up to four hours of the day plus he still had chores, work to be done once there. At such a young age, George was only getting about three and half hours of sleep daily. Staying over in town would not be a problem if someone else could pick up his slack around the farm.

George decided to speak to his Poppa about his situation. He told his father that he had fallen asleep at the scale counter a few time and the boss's son had awaken him. He was afraid that if it happens again it might mean losing the job as well as extra money the family needed so badly. Once he explained his position the matter was easily worked out. George knew that his Poppa did not want the extra money to stop coming in. After all, he received the pay each pay period, not George. George received a few cents of each dollar for his labor each pay period.

Several years went by with the same routine. George worked and his father collected the wages. George was not stupid to the fact that he was not getting what he deserved. He shared his dilemma with the boss's son, Jay, whom gave him some excellent advice he thought. Jay advised George to become his own man, work for himself and get paid fair wages for his worth. The best way to do that was to sever ties if necessary with the family's sharecropping business, step out own on his own. But! To accomplish this, he would first have to let Mr. Charles know that he would be moving out of the company storeroom. Next, he would have to ask the boss, Mr. Charles, if he could still continue to work for his company. If the boss's answer was yes, he should continue with a request that he would like his pay placed into his hands because he would no longer be working for his father. George took Jay's advice and ran with it.

The next morning, George hesitantly asked Mr. Charles for some time to talk to him about his employment future. Mr. Charles looked a bit puzzled but replied, "Now is good for me, let's talk." George, without any second thoughts, began telling of his situation. In addition, he told of what he wanted to accomplish. While listening to George, Mr. Charles wondered what took George so long to come to this logic. Mr. Charles responded with the statement, "No I do not a problem with any of your plans. If I can be of any more assistance just let me know."

George thanked Mr. Charles for the opportunities that have been given to him. He, however, did have a request. "Mr. Charles you can help me a lot. Now, I need a letter of character so I can secure a decent place to stay." "I can help you with that." Mr. Charles cheerfully replied. "You can pick up the letter at the end of the day tomorrow, not a problem." Mr. Charles continued with information that he need not have shared. "I am out of here; it has been a long day, good night." Mr. Charles turned waved his hand and exited the front door.

When the next pay period came around, George's Poppa came a knocking like clockwork. Once entering the warehouse, he went straight to the office of Mr. Charles thinking he was to collect wages from George's labor. Mr. Charles let Poppa know that the wages had been paid to George already. Poppa Will became so angry he had to turn his head away from Mr. Charles' direction and cuss under his breath. Several seconds passed before Poppa Will turned his head back in Mr. Charles direction and quickly sounded out "a good day to you Sir, " as he turned his entire body to exit the office. Shocked that he would not be receiving any money he quickly left the office. George's

Poppa was so mad he did not ask Mr. Charles if he knew the whereabouts of George.

After leaving the warehouse, being baffled, he just started walking. Several miles later, finally reaching the colored people neighborhood, is where he then happen to spot George. Seeing George looking nice and freshly dressed from head to toe, Poppa Will became even more confused. "This was not Sunday," he thought. As he looked more intently around the area, he knew his son's new address was impressive; the likes of those who lived well, educated colored folks surrounding. He began to wonder what was George doing to rate these accommodations. Was George now a hustler at night too? What has happen since he was seen last? Poppa Will said to himself out loud, "that boy better tell me something in a hurry" …

George knew this day would come. Anticipating his father's rage, he waited out front on the steps of his apartment house with two glasses and a tall bottle of bourbon. One of the glasses was full of dollar bills. Watching as his father approached swiftly, George stood up reached out his arms to greet his Poppa as he got closer. Once his father was in hearing distance, George acknowledged, "Glad to see my Poppa come have a drink with me." Seeing the glass of dollars actually slowed down the hostility George's poppa was feeling. Taking the glass from George hand, he then began to shake his head as if mystified. "Son, what is going on? Why are you here and not at the Mr. Charlie's barn?"

While clearing the glass, George responded, "Poppa I just had to leave that surrounding, I am a grown man. I need more than a hayloft for a bed. It is time for me to become my own man."

"Well son, if I would have known your plans, I would not have gone to the warehouse and been embarrassed. Matter of fact what are your grown up plans anyway? Are you planning to help the family any more, can we count on any help from you in the coming days?" George could only reply to his Poppa with a smile and a simple "YES! Now have a drink with me," George pleaded facing his Poppa with a relieved face. Filling the glasses with two fingers of Bourbon Whiskey all the while both men then sat down on the porch steps touching each other's raised glasses before downing the contents.

George and his Poppa talked for hours, talked about his future plans as they finished off the Bourbon. The spirited drinks loosen both men thoughts, opening up many topics. It seemed nothing was taboo, real talk, man to man talk that day. Poppa opened up and shared a lot about his dreams as well as his fears. Something George did not know about his father was his Poppa's hopes were that for each of his children to reach higher heights in life than he was able to ever reach. Poppa's dream was that none of them would remain in the fields picking crops all of their lives. One of Poppa's dreams was to purchase a tractor in the near future. With the tractor he could plow and harvest fields faster and the children would be able to attend school much more often. Poppa said he had been saving for years, saving for the acquisition of the tractor he had in mind. As George listened he began feeling better about his father. After having his wages taken for year's maybe something good came of this. But! George also knew people talked a lot when they were drinking booze. He hoped his father would walk the walk, not just talk the talk in the near future too.

After a while Poppa started babbling, saying the same thing over and over in a low muffled voice and leaning forward as if he would fall on his face. George recognized his father was intoxicated, wasted, so he helped him up the stairs and into his apartment. After putting Poppa to bed, George sat in his living room chair looking out the window. He was thinking that perhaps this has been the best day of his life, sharing dreams and hopes with his Poppa. How good was that?

Chapter 2: **BEING HIS OWN MAN**

Several weeks past and George started to feel a bit lonely. Missing his family had become more of a problem than he thought it would be. In the past, George would at least see his Poppa and maybe another family member when they came to pick up his wages. Being all grown up, an adult living alone is not all he thought it would be. George became lonely and bored. Now, with all the spare time and nothing to do George decided to venture out. He started walking the streets to see what he could see. As George walked, he noticed several Bars that served Caucasian people only. That is when a bright idea came into his head. George realized that he would never be successful unless he had something to call his own. What could that be? What would make money during any time of year? Knowing

Black folks like to have parties for almost any reason, especially with spirited drinks, George decided that he would set-up a Juke Joint in a back wooded area. An easy access location would be required. It would be a nice place for colored people to gather, have fun with relatives and friends and get their groove on if they please.

George had worked with Mr. Charlie's son Jay, for some time now. George had begun to trust Jay to the point of asking him for advice. George thought what it wouldn't hurt if he asked Jay a possibility question. After telling Jay of his idea and what was needed to get it off the ground, George listened to a silence for a few seconds. Suddenly a smile broke out on Jay face, and after a few more seconds a remark followed that surprised George totally. Jay expressed how he thought George had a great idea and he wanted to be a part of it. Jay said he knew of land in the outback that could be purchased for a small amount of capital. Jay continued with an offer that George did not have to think twice on. For 15 percent of the Juke Joints business, Jay would loan George the money to buy enough of the materials and the land to set up the Joint. However, George would have to pay Jay back the money that the land was obtained with.

Looking confused for a second George questioned Jay about one thing, if he had to repay Jay the money that the land was purchased with, to whom the land would belong. Jay began to laugh put his hand on George's shoulder and replied, "It will be all yours, you are my guy, my friend and I want to help in your vision. George, I will buy the land and sign it over to you, with you paying me five dollars a month until the price of the land is paid off." "Jay that sounds real good to me but! I need you to put that on paper just in case," George said agreeing. "Not a problem." Jay responded as he extended his hand to George.

"Jay, Now that our plan has been laid out, when will we be able to start this transaction? I am ready to get going as soon as possible. You know how I am about getting started with business." George explained. "I will look into it right away." Jay assured George.

A couple days later Jay retrieved money from the bank and began the acquisition of the outback land. George had already found a deal of thirty acres for a very good price in the outback off the main road. This purchase would also have to include a hundred feet of frontage access. Both knew the Juke Joint would need available entry access from the main road. With the land being purchased, George's idea was set in motion. His next step was to get lumber and fixtures to compliment the décor he had in mind. He also needed furnishing that would hold up to tough treatment in case a fight occurs. Tables and chairs getting thrown around hitting the floor had to be sturdy. The best place to get some pieces like that was to call on Granddad

Poppa Will. Poppa Will was the best carpenter in the tri-county area. When he built something it last. Mason jars would be good enough to drink out of, if somebody did not want to take their drinks from the bottle neck. Wanting to be a classy joint George's place had to have an outhouse nearby so patrons could relieve themselves without going into the woods. A potbelly stove for when it gets cold, a tin roof to guard against rain and shine, a juke box with all the latest sounds plus a wooden dance floor to dance on until blisters on your feet make you take a seat. Let's not forget petty young barmaids. What more is needed for a good time? On occasion live music from local musicians. Nothing feels better than that of a man owning his own business operation that is for sure.

Chapter 3: **AND LIFE BEGINS**

Having worked for another business minded person, it was now George's turn to run his own business. To get things done the way he wanted George had to give orders. This was something he was not accustom to doing, however, he became rather pleased with himself after seeing the results of his request. George recognized that getting his wishes done was easier when asked for help although the employees were paid. Knowing adults have chosen to work for him George showed his appreciation by rewarding them with praise. Understanding time is money George recognized that he did not have enough time in the day to complete the building of the Juke Joint. What was needed was someone to report back to him the progress of the workmen completing the construction. It did not take long for a person's name to come to mind. Little brother William would do very nicely. William used the nick-name Man, and he is the man for the job. Always being a talker this is just the interaction Man looked forward to. Being a Boss or Supervisor was just up Man's alley. He never had a problem letting anyone know of his likes or dislikes. Getting George's construction wishes followed could be an easy task that Man can handle. To sweeten the pot, George offered Man a percentage of the business. Agreeing to the deal, Man also discovered he would have to find good deals. Deals for boozes and furniture to supply the Joint plus become bartender-manager when George was away.

Building the Juke Joint in a dry county Man recognized the fact he had to locate some bootlegger supplier for liquor purchases. Bootleggers prices would be a lot more affordable; especially not having to go out of the county and pay state taxes. Man also needed to talk to George about paying off the Sheriff Deputies if any peace of mind was to be had during business operation hours. Man knew of the benefits and dangers of this kind of operation. Both pros and cons of this venue Man liked a lot. Man's biggest concern however was that of telling Poppa about his decision. His decision to work with George plus assuring Poppa that the crops in the fields would be taken care of without his presence was a big apprehension. Man needed to figure out a smooth and safe way of telling Poppa.

In the meantime, the effort to complete the current task of building the Joint had to be handled. …But, a timetable to open the Joint had not been established so that had to be discussed. Man's thinking was that the building could be finished in two or three days if work was done on the weekend, something he did not have a problem with. The crew of workers George had hired was not up to speed as far as Man was concern, so he let them go, fired them. Man knew of people who worked faster and for far less pay, and did quality carpentry work. Man not wanting to burn bridges called the guys George hired and told them they would not be needed anymore for this project. To the men's surprise, Man let them know each would be paid for the remainder of the day. With that being said, it smoothed some of the negative reactions down. Man knew he would need these men again, be it work or as customers. Being a Mason Brother himself, he knew the importance of the builder trade always helping a brother when possible. Shutting down the building operations for the day Man decided to head for town to discuss the events of the day. George had to be told of the situations and changes made at the Juke Joint's site. So! Right away Man made his way to town to inform George.

George's shift at the warehouse had come to an end just after dark. While locking up the front windows and door to the building he noticed Man standing across the street under a streetlight. First thing to come to mind for

George was Man was here with some bad news. Catching each other's eyes, George waved his hand to Man. Man responded by doing the same. Mr. Charles had left earlier in the day so George was locking up the warehouse alone. After completing his task quickly, George walked over to Man and asked if everything was alright. Man replied with a smile and nodded with an up and down movement of the head. "Hey Brother let's go get a drink. There are a few things I want to talk to you about." Man subjected. George face showed relief right after hearing Man's answer and request. "Okay, not a problem, "I am fine with that." George answered. "Brother, we can go up to my room. I have a little something, something there." George informed Man. "Solid," Man replied; adding "if you are waiting on me then you are backing up, let's go my throat is dry."

Once they reached the apartment house, Man took 2 steps at a time up the stairs. Arriving at the door of George's room, Man entered as if he lived there. George just smiled as he told his brother to make himself to home, meaning get what you want. Without hesitation, Man headed to the cupboard area, opened the cabinet door, got a glass jar from the top shelf then opened the bottom door to retrieve the booze. Not thinking to ask if George wanted a jar to drink with, Man instead asked, "Why do you keep the booze down low, not up high with the glasses brother? George responded with a smile then a sarcastic "yes, I am going to join you with a drink, thanks for the glass." Knowing that is not the question asked of him. From the tone of George voice Man quickly caught on that his brother felt forgotten. "Oh! Sorry Baby George, I will get you a glass. I did not think you were going to join me." Baby George was the nickname George was called as a Boy. He did not like it then, and he surely did not care for it now. A grown ass man being called baby just did not sit right with George. "Man if you call me that one more time, I am not

Jerry Powell

playing I am going to kick the mess out of you, got that?" George told his brother with a straight face. "Take it easy brother; can't you take a little ribbing?" Man said with a hearty laugh. "You are always going to be my big baby!" Man continued as he leaned over to George, quickly rubbed his brother's cheek. "Stop this foolishness." George interrupted, "you said you had something to talk to me about so get to it." George said in a no nonsense tone. Man looked at his brother then took a sip of liquor from the jar, placed it on the table and began to tell George of his ideas for the Juke Joint.

After a few more drinks and several hours of talking the stage was set. Man and George had worked out what they thought was the perfect combination. Location, building, entertainment, boozes and security, everything seems to be lining up real nicely. An opening to be in 3 weeks, right around the 4th of July holiday weekend, what could be better. George having learned to become a good businessperson knew he had to keep Man's interest high. So! He told Man to hold out his arm and open his hand. He then placed 5 one dollar bills in Man's hand. Man, surprised at the action, asked what this was for. "It is for you brother, for all the hard work you have been putting into our project. Go buy you some clothes and start looking like the boss. Now please do not buy those clothes that make you look like a peacock. We want to be business like in all of our affairs."

Man looked at his brother for a few seconds before his words could exit his mouth. "George, I am so proud to be your brother; you are taking us to a place that once was only a dream. Thanks for letting me share this experience with you." "Man, we have been on this journey together for a long time so it is time to make it worthwhile. Let's stick together and make this business happen." George then stood up from his seat walked to the other side of the table; positioned his left hand on Man's shoulder, extended his right hand to shake. In his mind this was sealing the deal. Right away Man stood to his feet with his right hand extended reaching for his brothers' hand. "Let us do this damn thing!" Man loudly boasted while shaking hands with George.

Chapter 4: **WHAT YOU CALL ME THAT FOR?**

The Juke Joint was the place to get intoxicated, meet women, gamble and attain all kinds of thrills. Further out in the back woods is where the alcohol cooker, Moonshiners, tried to hide their sights and smell of the cooking stills. However, if one didn't see the smoke you could easily smell the odor of the corn being cooked. Corn liquor was one of the best crops produced in Collin County, Mississippi. One thing about that Mississippi Corn Mash when drinking it, it sure rolled down the throat gently. Because of the effortless smooth swallowing of the liquor, many customers, before they knew it, became higher than a kite. 150 Proof Corn that is 75% alcohol will have a special effect on drinkers. They will get drunk in a hurry.

Loud talking and trying to sing over each other was common practice at Studd's Juke Joint. The customers, mostly field hands, seemed just happy to be alive. Hugging and kissing everyone they knew and not worrying about tomorrow, today. After a few drinks to get their minds right, the dance floor would get packed. Most dancers forgot about their relaxed hair styles, which took hours to have done. They would start to swing each other into the air trying to outperform the others. When the music slowed down, dancing cheek to cheek was the next best thing to being in bed. Slow dancing and some smart conversation often lead to becoming sexual merriment. Being handsome, lightly brown skinned and not tide down, you had a good likelihood of scoring cherished time with one of the permissive cuties. There were no extra rooms in Stud's Joint so if you had thought about getting lucky, the woods would have to be the destination to get down and share body fluids.

George Freeman was a righteous kind of guy. One not to try and take all of a hard working field hands money, he would see customers getting out of control and cut-off their drinks. George would have his bartender give them food and coffee to help sober them up. George was a smart businessperson. He did not want people to get drunk, which usually lead to trouble. George knew if a person was out of commission in jail, sick and not able to return, his profits would be less. George believed that treating a person with respect wins their favor. That way a person will be glad to do business day after day. At the same time, George did not allow anyone to try and punk him. He had large hands and a big stick and wasn't afraid to use them. Many men can attest to that.

George's popularity was county wide. He also had several women on the side that he personally entertained. George's belief was that of the old testament of the King James Bible. That a man should had as many women as he could afford. Now that didn't mean he married each of his children's mama. However, George did not disclaim any that he thought he had a part in bringing into this world. Some say George has enough children to form a football team. That is how he received his nickname … "STUDD"

The Juke Joints opening weekend came faster than George and Man would have liked. When July 4th arrived the Joint was not ready. However! The show must go on is the saying in the entertainment business and now their entertainers. At the Juke Joint, not the entire electric system had been installed. No lights, no electric power means working with candles and that could be a problem. Darken areas in the woods you do not want, especially not entering or exit the property. It is hard enough to control games of chance with lights. For opening night, George and Man put their heads together and decided that extra outside security was need. Each of them wanted at the end of the night, for all the talk to be about the good time and pleasure they had at Studd's place. A successful opening weekend would include no injury or customers robbed of their winnings.

Word got out swiftly of the good times had at the Juke Joint and soon there was standing room only in the club. Being a successful club owner came with perks. All the time women would throw themselves into George arms. George being a young man sure liked the attention he received and took advantage of his opportunities. After being with several women and having relations with them, after a short period and many relationships, George developed a name for himself. Not one to stick with any one woman for very long George became known as Studd. A man that is popular with the ladies. The women all knew of each other however, for whatever reason they could not stay away. The hush-hush of George's exploits with the women is still a mystery. The woman would not tell what caused them to give in to George's advances. They just smiled at each other as they passed one another. Studd became a legend in the area. ...But! Just that claim to fame George did not want. George had other plans for himself, ones that included becoming a much larger landowner and businessperson.

During George's routine business days at the Warehouse, he became quite friendly with many important people in the county, political and the likes. George began to have dreams of vast wealth and properties. The County Clerk visited the warehouse often; he was a good friend of Mr. Charles. Knowing the right people to purchase stuff in Mississippi is half the battle. To buy flat black bottom land in Mississippi the right connection had to be in place. For George's vision of the future to happen it sometimes included sharing a bit of cash and in some cases helping county officials wanting introductions to agreeable females. With the help of some of the officials, George was able to make things happen the way he hoped. George had to give up a lot to get his agenda done. "Fair exchange is not robbery" was George's model. George's thoughts for his future persisted as days passed. Soon after the purchase of more land and a house, George's estate seemed to be headed in the right direction. After a while it seemed as if George had it all; respect, money, women and properties. However, George felt as if a part of his life success was not compete. But what was missing was a wife, one that he could start his own family ancestry with. Now George must decide what in a women can he live with or live without. Decisions for the future now the searches for George's companion for life are beginning …

Jerry Powell

Special thanks to my family and friends for your support and encouragement as I ventured on this literary journey.

www.ingramcontent.com/pod-product-compliance
Lightning Source LLC
Chambersburg PA
CBHW050916120626
46552CB00004B/1605